The Pout-Pout Fish
and the
Worry-Worry
Whale

Deborah Diesen
Pictures by **Isidre Monés**

Farrar Straus Giroux
New York

For all my fellow worriers —D.D.

Farrar Straus Giroux Books for Young Readers
An imprint of Macmillan Publishing Group, LLC
120 Broadway, New York, NY 10271 • mackids.com

Our books may be purchased in bulk for promotional, educational, or business use.
Please contact your local bookseller or the Macmillan Corporate and Premium Sales Department
at (800) 221-7945 ext. 5442 or by email at MacmillanSpecialMarkets@macmillan.com.

Library of Congress Cataloging-in-Publication Data is available.

First edition, 2022
Book design by Aram Kim and Melisa Vuong
Color separations by Embassy Graphics
Printed in China by RR Donnelley Asia Printing Solutions Ltd., Dongguan City, Guangdong Province

ISBN 978-0-374-38930-7 (hardcover)
10 9 8 7 6 5 4 3

BIRTHDAY PARTY

Mr. Fish was quite excited.
"There's a party to attend!"
With gift in hand, he headed out,
Then bumped into a friend.

"Hello there, Willa Whale," he said.
"We're off to the same place!"
But his friend did not look happy.
There was *worry* on her face.

"Is something wrong?" asked Mr. Fish.
"I'd like to help, if so."
"It's the party," answered Willa Whale.
"I *don't* want to go!"

Is worry even bigger,
Even bigger than a whale?

"I told them I was coming.
But then I got to thinking
Of countless things that might go wrong.
Now my tummy's sinking!

"What if it's too crowded?
Or no one wants to play?
What if I feel out of place
And don't know what to say?"

Mr. Fish was understanding.
"Sometimes I worry, too!
Worry tells us stories—
But not all of them are true.

"So take a great big breath with me,
To soften worry's voice.
Then pick one thing, *just one*, to try—
A tiny little choice."

*Maybe worry isn't bigger,
Isn't bigger than a whale.*

Willa thought this over.
"I could go . . . for just the *start*.
If all my worries *do* come true,
I know I can depart."

With plan in mind, the two good friends
Continued on their way.
Deep breaths and conversation
Helped keep worried thoughts at bay.

Closer to the party
Willa's worry started churning.
But then she heard, "You've got this!"
And she felt her calm returning.

The place was loud and crowded,
But she found a comfy space.
She watched her friends and played a bit,
Less worry on her face.

Maybe worry isn't bigger,
Isn't bigger than a whale!

Willa didn't talk a lot.
She felt a little shy.
"But that's okay," she coached herself.
"I only have to *try*."

When worries started bubbling up,
She breathed and whooshed them out.
"You're doing great!" said Mr. Fish.
It helped dispel her doubt.

But all at once, her peace of mind
Upended in a burst.
The time had come for *singing*—
"And my singing is *the worst!*

"What if I'm too squeaky?
Off-key and awfully rude?
What if I forget the words?
What if I get *booed!*"

Worry's growing bigger,
Even **bigger** than a whale!

A flood of worried thinking
Cascaded through her head.
It nearly overwhelmed her—
But she *made a plan* instead.

She turned and said to Mr. Fish,
"I'm going to try *one note*.
If I get stuck, I'll hum instead.
I'll let the music float."

So Willa tried . . . She sang her note!
The voices joined as one!
And Willa Whale *enjoyed* herself.
"This party has been fun!

"Worry tells us stories,
But not all of them are true.
So when worry swims inside me,
There are things that I can do.

"I can *find a friend to talk to*,

Then *breathe and make a plan*,

And *choose a tiny step to take*—

Believe and know I can!"

"Because worry **isn't** bigger,
Isn't bigger than a whale!"